Ninja Nico: Ultimate Ninja Warrior Road Trip

Marcy Nicole

DEDICATION

To my Ninja Nico and Mighty Mia,
Always do your best and follow your dreams!
Love, Mommy

ACKNOWLEDGMENTS

Thank you to my ninja warrior family – Gino, Nico, and Mia – for all of your inspiration.

Thank you to the ninja warrior coaches who are helping make the real Ninja Nico's dreams come true!

Ryan
Therese
Phil
Tamara
Malcolm
Ian
Dave
Elaina
Lauren
Xander
Declan
Ryan
Saad

CHAPTER 1

"It's almost time!" Nico shouted, as he bounced off the kitchen wall like a parkour master.

"Relax, the show doesn't start for another thirty minutes," said Nico's mom. "And please wipe off your shoe marks from my kitchen wall."

Nico was always leaving marks on the walls throughout his family's house as he imagined it was his own, personal obstacle course. He spider-climbed the hallways and hung from the archways over the doors. He basically navigated his way through the house like in the sport of parkour, jumping and vaulting off everything to get from one room to another.

His mom supported his ninja-warrior trait of not being able to sit still, but she didn't appreciate the dirt, handprints, and footprints left behind from his moves. It became a ritual for Nico to grab a wet towel and wipe down his tracks at the end of each day.

"Sorry, mom, I'll clean it up tonight after the show," Nico whined.

"We have company walking in any minute," his mom reminded him. "I'd like the house to look decent for at least an hour today."

The company included Nico's grandparents, aunt, uncle, cousins, friends, and some of his ninja warrior coaches and teammates. One teammate in particular was his neighbor and best friend, Riley.

His other neighbors and best friends, Jacob and Ryder, were supportive of Nico and Riley and their ninja warrior competitions, but they were content hanging out at home and playing their video games. Even with Nico's backyard ninja course close by, they still didn't get in to the sport. Riley came over every chance she got to practice her skills for free on the course that Nico's dad built.

There was a time where Riley snuck into Nico's yard at night to use the obstacle course. She couldn't really afford to train at a ninja gym, plus she didn't want her friends making fun of her for trying out the sport and possibly failing at being a ninja. Now she trains a couple of days at Great Obstacles, Nico's ninja warrior gym. Riley's mom worked out a payment plan with Coach Daniel, who is the owner and head coach. And the rest of the week she hangs out on Nico's course. His dad is constantly making changes to the backyard course and adding new obstacles, so Riley and Nico can keep improving their ninja skills.

Riley also brought some of her family over with her to the viewing party, as she was also on the show. She walked in the door with her mom, carrying a fruit tray and brownies.

"I'll take those off your hands," Nico joked, as he grabbed the brownies.

"I'll take those," Nico's mom said as she snatched the treats from her son. "Go and visit with your friends and I'll let you know when the snacks are set up."

"You mean, my fans?" Nico laughed, as he walked into the family room. He was wearing a Ninja Nico shirt, which his mom had made up for the TV competition. His grandparents, who were on the couch anxiously waiting in front of the TV, were each sporting a Ninja Nico shirt.

His friends, Ryder and Jacob, were seated on the floor, but they were wearing *Ultimate Ninja* shirts. *Ultimate Ninja* is the video game version of ninja warrior, which they preferred to play.

"I just want to know how you and Riley did on this TV competition," Ryder said, barely looking up from his phone.

"Yeah, did you fall on the first obstacle?" Jacob joked.

"I'm sure Nico did excellent," his Grandma chimed in, winking at her grandson.

"You must have made the blooper reel, with those classic Nico falls," Ryder added. "You always seem to have entertaining dismounts from the obstacles. I was just watching some of your team's videos online. You should be a stunt man."

Riley joined the kids in the family room.

"Did you guys watch the video from last month where Nico fell down like a tree and Coach Jake yelled 'Timber!' from the sidelines?" asked Riley.

"That was a good one," laughed Jacob. "I can't wait to see how you both did on the TV show. Can't you just give us a hint?"

"You'll just have to watch and see," Riley laughed.

CHAPTER 2

Two months ago, before the TV show was filmed …

"Nico, we need to leave for the gym," yelled his Dad. "This is your last practice before we hit the road, so you should make the most of it!"

Nico had been training hard for his upcoming competitive appearance on *The Ultimate Kid Ninja Competition*. The show was being filmed in Orlando, Florida, so Nico and his family were about to take a road trip from the Midwest to the South. His friend, Riley, was also competing on the show, so her family was going to join them as well.

As Nico and his dad headed out the door, his mom handed him his bag which included his ninja shoes, a water bottle, and a protein bar.

"You guys have fun at the gym," said his mom sarcastically. "I'll just be here doing laundry and packing up suitcases for our road trip."

"OK, we will!" joked Nico.

Once Nico was at Great Obstacles, his ninja warrior gym, he quickly ran to warm up with his friends. Riley was doing jumping jacks with Coach Mia, while Joey was pretending to do jumping jacks.

"Joey, you need to put a little more effort in it," yelled Coach Mia.

"I don't see how jumping jacks are going to help me win a TV competition," whined Joey.

"You need to warm up your muscles before you start training for your TV competition," added Riley.

"You can do all the jumping jacks you want, Joey," said Nico. "But you'll never beat me in the competition!"

"I think they should be called 'jumping Jakes'," chimed in Coach Jake as he jumped in front of the kids.

"Why does everything have to be about you?" Riley teased.

"Well, you better get used to calling them that," Coach Jake teased back. "Because we are going to be doing lots of 'jumping Jakes' at every rest stop we hit along the road!"

"What are you talking about?" Riley asked.

"Yeah, I didn't get a chance to tell you yet, Riley, but Coach Jake is coming along on our road trip to Orlando," Nico declared. "Since there is room in my mom's SUV, he is driving with us."

"Yeah, I guess there would be room in the car since it is only my mom and I joining you guys," said Riley, a bit teary-eyed. "I guess I was holding out hope that my dad would be home in time for the taping of *The Ultimate Kid Ninja Competition*."

"Aw, Riley, I'm so sorry," said Coach Mia as she hugged her. "It must be hard having your dad in the military. I know he is gone a lot."

"He has been gone a year, but his tour is almost over," Riley said. "We just don't know exactly when he will be back in Michigan for good."

"Riley, we are going to have an awesome road trip," Coach Jake said excitedly. "And you'll have lots of people cheering you on when you compete."

"And both of our moms cheer loud enough to sound like a mob of fans," Nico laughed.

"Very true," said Riley, smiling again. "My mom definitely makes up for my dad not being there."

"Your mom is awesome, Riley," said Coach Mia. "I wish I was going with you guys on this trip. It will be a fun group. And with Coach Jake along for the ride, there will never be a dull moment."

"I can't wait to drive through the Rocky Mountains," Riley

said, perking up again. "I've never been in that part of the country."

"It's the Smoky Mountains we'll be driving through," Nico said, correcting her. "The Rocky Mountains are in Colorado. That would be way out of our way to drive through them."

"OK, I mean the Smoky Mountains," Riley said, glaring at Nico. "Whatever mountains are in Tennessee. I've never driven through there."

"If there is snow on the mountains, then I'm bringing my snow board!" Coach Jake said excitedly.

"Jake, we aren't going to have time for snowboarding," said Riley. "Plus, I don't think there will be snow on the mountains in the summer."

"Some mountains have really high elevation, so there is snow all year," Nico explained. "I don't think we'll see any in the Smoky Mountains, though. I'll do some research before we leave and see what we can expect in that region."

Nico studied the weather as a hobby and hoped to be a meteorologist one day.

"OK you future TV stars, we need to get back to warming up and training," Coach Mia said firmly. "You only have a few days before the big competition."

And the kids immediately went back to their stretching and 'jumping Jakes' and got ready for an intense workout on the gym's obstacle course, which Coach Daniel had set up special just for them.

Once Nico was back home, he watched videos online of ninja warrior competitions with his dad. They reviewed footage for a few hours, focusing on the skills used by competitors on different obstacles. Every course was different when it came to the sport of ninja warrior. So, Nico wanted to be prepared as best as he could with every type of obstacle imaginable.

"I wonder how tall their warped wall will be?" Nico thought out loud.

"Well, considering your age group, I would assume it would be about 12 feet. And since you've been able to reach the top of the 14-foot wall, you should have no problem," Nico's dad said encouragingly.

"I just can't wait to hit that buzzer," Nico said as he imagined himself reaching the end of the obstacle course and hitting the infamous buzzer. He pictured his family and friends cheering him on while wearing their Ninja Nico shirts.

This was going to be epic. Nico couldn't wait to hit the road for Orlando and reach his goal of winning *The Ultimate Kid Ninja Competition.*

CHAPTER 3

The day of the road trip, Nico jumped out of bed and swung from the rings hanging in his doorway.

"Let's hit the road!" he yelled to his parents.

"We are almost ready to hit the road," said his mom, walking over to give him a hug. "I'm so proud of you for this journey."

"Our journey hasn't started yet, we need to get in the car," Nico laughed.

"You know what I mean," his mom said. "You have been working really hard in your ninja warrior training. And I am beyond proud of you. Win or lose on this TV competition, you are my favorite ninja warrior ever!"

"Thanks, Mom," Nico said, blushing. "However, let's only use the word 'win' on this road trip! I can't have any negative thoughts in my head."

"Yes, sir!" his mom laughed. "You know I'll be cheering the loudest!"

"You'll also have Coach Jake and Riley's mom to compete with on cheering loud," laughed Nico.

"Oh, I will 'win' a yelling competition every time!" his mom said proudly. "Speaking of Jake, I think I hear him outside with Dad."

"Awesome!" Nico said as he ran for the front door.

"Pace yourself, kid," said his mom. "You are still in your pajamas."

Nico looked down at his clothing and laughed.

"Well, at least I'll be comfy for the long road trip!" he laughed.

Nico ran back to his room to change and gather his bags. His mom helped him pack clothing for the trip, but he also packed a bag for the car ride with his electronics, chargers, and even a couple of books to read.

Nico had a reading list from the library's summer reading program and planned to read as many books as possible. There was a prize involved for reaching 40 hours of reading for the summer, so he figured he'd get in lots of hours while on the road trip. Even though the prize was usually just a puzzle or a book, Nico enjoyed winning anything.

From the time he was little, he turned everything into a competition. He got that trait from his grandpa. At 3 years old, Nico had to battle to beat his grandpa at card games. Grandpa played to win, even if it meant beating out his little grandson at Go Fish and Poker. Nico inherited that same mentality of victory.

Nico played soccer and tennis throughout his whole childhood. He also earned a black belt in Tae Kwon Do when he was 8 years old. At charity events held at his martial arts school, he won contests for the most push-ups and holding a squat the longest.

The sport of ninja warrior has been perfect for Nico. He thrives in the environment of challenging courses and racing against a clock. He has watched *The Ultimate Ninja Competition* on TV with his family since he was little, while making an obstacle course out of the couch and chairs around the TV. Now he had his chance to be on the kid version of the show and it was a dream come true.

After about a half hour of packing and re-packing the car, with the addition of suitcases and bags from Riley and her mom, they were ready to go. There were enough seats for everyone in Nico's mom's SUV, but with a week's worth of luggage for six people there wasn't much floor space. Nico's dad managed to fit bags into every nook and cranny of the SUV.

"I call shotgun!" yelled Coach Jake.

"Actually, I thought the grownups could take turns sitting

in the front seat. To start off, though, my wife and I are going to drive and navigate in the front seat. You'll get a turn eventually," Nico's dad laughed.

As the vehicle pulled out of the driveway and drove down the street, Nico took a look back at his backyard obstacle course and then the playground at the school. He couldn't believe that all of the time he spent playing and training there would lead him to where he was headed today.

"I feel like this is a dream," Nico said under his breath.

Just then, Coach Jake reached over and pinched him on the arm.

"Ow!" yelled Nico. "What was that for?"

"You are supposed to pinch someone when they think they are dreaming, to show them physical proof that they aren't," explained Coach Jake.

"I think that is more of an expression to pinch someone when they are dreaming, Jake! Not to actually pinch them," Nico complained.

"Wow, are you guys already fighting back there?" Nico's mom asked.

"This is going to be a long road trip," Riley's mom jokingly chimed in.

"When are we going to stop for food?" asked Coach Jake.

"Jake, we just got on the road," said Nico's dad.

"This is going to be a really, really long road trip," laughed Nico's mom.

After about a half hour of driving, the group met up with another family in a shopping center parking lot. The two vehicles were following each other from Michigan to Florida, while the families of other kids they knew who were going to be on the show (like Joey and Megan from Great Obstacles) were heading to Orlando via airplane.

"I see Dylan's family over there," Nico shouted, pointing to a black SUV in the parking lot.

Dylan and his younger brother, Jordan, were also contestants on *The Ultimate Kid Ninja Competition*. Their dad, Coach Jon, owns a ninja warrior gym, Hang Tough, located about a half hour from Great Obstacles. This past spring, Hang Tough had water damage from frequent storms in the area. So, Dylan, Jordan, and some other ninjas from Hang Tough trained at Great Obstacles for a while. Nico was at first intimidated by Dylan, but they eventually became friends when everyone worked together to repair Dylan's backyard obstacle course, which was damaged in another storm.

Dylan and Jordan waved from the back seat of their car, while Nico's parents got out to talk to Dylan's parents about the long ride ahead.

Dylan rolled down his window and motioned for Nico to

do the same.

"We are going to get to Orlando first," yelled Dylan, who was always competing with Nico.

"No way!" shouted Nico. "My dad is going to be the lead car, so we'll beat you!"

"I think we'll get there at the same time," Riley said, trying to be grown up and keep the peace.

"No, we'll definitely get there first!" yelled Coach Jake.

Riley just shook her head at the competitive boys.

CHAPTER 4

After about three hours in the car, the kids were getting restless. And they weren't the only ones.

"Are we there yet?" whined Coach Jake.

"Ninjas can't sit still this long," chimed in Nico.

"I second that," added Riley.

The parents all looked at each other and Nico's mom nodded that she would answer them back.

"No, we are not even close to being there," she said. "And we are well aware that ninjas can't sit still very long. We have breaks planned on this trip; however, we need to go more than a couple of hours at a time or we'll never get to Florida."

"I definitely need a break from driving soon, but I wanted to get in one more hour before I stop," explained Nico's dad. "Plus, I'm not quite ready to fill up the gas tank again.

Another hour on the road would be great."

"But Nico has to use the bathroom," said Coach Jake.

"No, I don't," Nico barked back.

Coach Jake nudged him, as Nico realized he was trying to get the parents to stop sooner.

"Ah yes, I have to go really bad," laughed Nico.

"You kids are impossible," laughed Nico's mom. "And Jake, you are worse than the kids."

Everyone laughed as Nico's dad agreed that he would make a stop sooner. Nico's mom called Coach Jon in the other vehicle and his family agreed that a stop soon would be great.

"You wouldn't believe how much my kids are whining," Coach Jon said.

"Oh, I have a pretty good idea," laughed Nico's mom. "And Jake is just as bad as the kids!"

When the two vehicles pulled off the freeway for a break, they looked for a restaurant to have lunch. Except, nobody could agree on where to eat.

"I want pizza," said Riley.

"Sub sandwiches, please," chimed in Nico.

"Tacos!" yelled Coach Jake.

Dylan's family had the same problem agreeing on where to eat. So, they decided on a family-style diner that was sure to have a variety of food for everyone.

Except, once they walked inside, they discovered that the diner was disgusting. The floors were covered in crumbs and dirt, and the tables were sticky. And when Riley and her mom went into the restroom, they came back out quickly, plugging their noses.

"Nope," said Riley's mom. "We are not staying here."

Everyone agreed that they needed to find somewhere else to eat. On the way out the door, Nico's shoes were sticking to the floor from all the grime on the ground.

"Maybe you should try walking on the walls, Nico," teased his mom as she helped him out the door. "Except, those don't look much cleaner than the floors."

"At least my shoes now have good traction to climb the walls!" laughed Nico. "I need to run up a warped wall right now! I bet I'd make 16 feet easily."

"You couldn't make 16 feet on a warped wall wearing any kind of shoes," joked Dylan, who loved to tease Nico about his ninja warrior skills. The two friends were very competitive, but also very supportive of each other.

"I really need to use a restroom and I'm super hungry," said Riley, changing the topic back to finding a restaurant.

"How about we try that restaurant across the street?" asked

Dylan's mom, pointing to another tiny restaurant.

"Not unless we look it up online first," laughed Coach Jon. "We are not making that mistake again."

Everyone started scrolling through their phones to look up the other restaurants in the area for customer reviews and menus. They decided on a pizzeria chain that they were all familiar with and everyone was happy with the choice, except Coach Jake.

"Jake, we'll get your tacos at the next stop," said Nico's mom, treating Jake like one of the kids.

"Thanks, mom," laughed Coach Jake.

Nico's mom took the next shift of driving, which meant she was the one to pick the music playing in the car. This meant a few hours of boy bands, movie songs, and songs from the 1980s.

"How much longer do we have to listen to your 'oldies' songs, Mom?" Nico whined.

"These aren't 'oldies' songs, but the songs I grew up with," his mom explained.

"Yes, 'old' music, so it is called 'oldies'," Nico added. "These are songs from like the 1900s."

"No, they aren't," chimed in Riley's mom. "Oh wait, yes they are."

"Well still, they aren't that old. The music your

grandparents listened to, now those songs are 'oldies' from like the 1950s and 1960s," Nico's mom clarified.

"No, those are 'really oldies'," laughed Nico, joined by the rest of the car.

After another hour or so of listening to the music on Nico's mom's playlist, it was time to figure out where to stop for dinner. Nico's dad started looking up restaurants on his phone that would be located at the next few exits off the freeway. Coach Jake was sure to remind him that they were going to get tacos.

All that was available was a fast-food taco place, so they picked up an order at the drive-through window for Jake and the kids. The adults decided to get chicken sandwiches and salads at the place next door, so they picked those up and everyone ate in the cars.

After about 5 minutes of eating, Nico spilled his drink all over Riley. The moms frantically wiped it up using the cheap, fast-food napkins, which tore apart and didn't absorb much of the spill.

"Thanks a lot, Nico!" shouted Riley. "Now I look like I wet my pants."

Just then, a noise came from the way-back of the car, where Coach Jake was seated. The noise was followed by an awful smell.

"Eww, yuck! It stinks in here," said Riley. "Put the windows down, please!"

Everyone looked back at Coach Jake, who was laughing.

"I guess the tacos weren't such a great idea," he joked.

"Oh my gosh, get me out of this car," wailed Riley. "I can't stand it anymore. I'm so glad I don't have brothers."

The boys just laughed as Riley begged to know how much longer until they would arrive at a hotel for the night.

CHAPTER 5

After a long day of driving, the two carloads decided to stop at a hotel for the night.

As the parents went and checked in at the front desk, the kids and Coach Jake got out of the car to stretch and do their 'jumping Jakes'. They knocked on the window of Dylan's car, where Dylan and his brother, Jordan, were asleep. That just made them knock harder.

Dylan suddenly sat up and looked startled as he stared out the window. He wiped drool from his mouth and rolled down his window.

"Oh, I wish I would have taken a picture of you like that," laughed Nico. "That could come in handy one day."

"Very funny," said Dylan. "What's up?"

"We can't sit in the car any longer," said Coach Jake. "So, we are going to check out this hotel. Come on!"

Dylan and Jordan jumped at the chance to get out of their car.

The boys all started wrestling with each other as they scampered across the lawn.

"More boys," laughed Riley. "I wish Coach Mia could have joined us on this trip instead."

"What for? Don't you enjoy my company?" teased Coach Jake.

"You know you are awesome, Coach Jake," said Riley. "It would just be nice to have another girl on this trip, aside from our moms."

Just then, Riley glanced over the fence, where a playground sat in a park like a shining ninja star.

"Forget your silly wrestling, it is ninja time!" yelled Riley, as she broke out into a sprint toward the playground.

The boys promptly followed her, with everyone racing each other to the climbing structure.

"I won!" yelled Riley, who reached the playground first. She threw her arms in the air for victory.

"No fair, you had a head start," whined Jordan.

"Stop whining and start climbing," Dylan told his younger brother.

The kids spent the next 10 minutes swinging from the

monkey bars, climbing up the poles on the swing set, and trying to see how far they could lache (swinging forward from one object to another, using your body as momentum) off the chin-up bars and onto the dirt below. They marked their distances in the dirt with a stick, trying to outdo each other. Coach Jake had made it the farthest.

Suddenly the kids heard their parents yelling at them.

"There you are!" shouted Dylan's mom. "We thought something happened to you."

"Well, we assumed that Coach Jake was with all of you," said Nico's mom, giving Jake a dirty look. "But we had no clue where you went. This complex is huge."

"Had we known there was a playground next door, we would have looked there first," laughed Nico's dad.

"Why didn't you call my phone?" Dylan asked his dad.

"I did call your phone, but then I heard it ringing in the back seat of the car," Coach Jon scolded his son. "You also left the car running, with the keys in the ignition."

"Oops," said Dylan.

"You are lucky nobody took off with our car," Coach Jon added. "Then we'd never get to the ninja TV competition."

"Sweet! Then I wouldn't have to compete against Dylan!" yelled Nico.

Nico's dad gave him a look that implied he better not say

anything more.

"Where's my mom?" Riley asked, noticing her mom wasn't with the other parents.

"Oh, she had to make a phone call," said Nico's mom.

Riley wondered who her mom could have possibly been calling.

Once the parents were settled into their hotel rooms for the night, the kids and Coach Jake met up in the hallway to raid the vending machine.

As they walked down the hallway of the hotel, Nico tried to spider-climb the walls. His arms and legs weren't long enough to reach both sides at the same time, though, and he landed face first onto the carpet.

"Ha, I'm taller! I got this," said Coach Jake as he tried to jump onto the wall with both feet. Except, he also couldn't reach and made an epic fall.

"Copycat," Nico teased.

Nico was the one known for epic falls on the ninja course, playgrounds, and pretty much anywhere he climbed or hung from stuff, which was pretty much everywhere. He always managed to either land on his feet or tuck and roll gracefully.

"You guys need to both quit banging on the walls and

falling on the ground," scolded Riley. "You are going to get us kicked out of the hotel."

"That won't get us kicked out of the hotel," Dylan joined in. "This might, though!"

He jumped up and grabbed a light fixture on the wall, attempting to reach the next one with his long arms. He also fell, making a thud on the ground.

"Can you ninja a little quieter?" Riley laughed.

"How about this?" asked Nico, as he started walking on his hands down the hallway. He was joined by Dylan and Jordan.

Right behind them, and attempting to kick it up a notch, Coach Jake did a back handspring and then a back flip. As he tumbled upside down, his coins for the vending machine tumbled out of his pocket.

"Money!" yelled Jordan, who flipped back onto his feet and dove toward Coach Jake and his pile of change on the floor.

"I wouldn't do that if I were you," laughed Nico.

"Yeah, don't mess with Coach Jake," added Riley.

Jordan ignored both kids and started picking up the loose change and putting it in his pockets. Coach Jake then grabbed him by the ankles and hung him upside down. As a result, all of his coins, plus the change he stole from

Coach Jake, fell to the ground.

"Money!" shouted Dylan, Nico, and Riley, diving to the floor and mocking Jordan.

The kids continued to laugh down the hallway toward the vending machine. When they reached the tall structure at the end of the hallway, they read an out-of-order sign.

"Great! Now how are we supposed to get snacks?" asked Jordan.

"We just need to find a machine on another floor," said Nico. "Or we can head to the gift shop next to the lobby. I'm sure they have some snacks."

Jordan started to walk toward the elevator, but the rest of the crew ventured down the stairway.

"Ninjas take the stairs!" Dylan yelled to his brother.

Coach Jake and the kids went down the stairway just like ninja warriors. They hung onto the railing, lifted their legs off the ground, and used a hand-over-hand motion to work their way down the stairs. Jordan opted to leap down a couple of stairs at a time, in which Coach Jake quickly stopped him.

"We are ninjas, but we are careful," scolded Coach Jake. "I don't want to end up in the emergency room tonight with any of you. And a broken ankle would put a damper on your chance of winning, or even competing on, the TV competition."

Jordan then walked down the stairs carefully, over emphasizing each step he took with care. Coach Jake just gave him a harsh look and then broke into laughter.

The group continued on toward the gift shop, where the kids happily indulged in snacks that they got to pick out for themselves. There were no protein bars or trail mix. Instead, the kids grabbed chips, cookies, and everything else their parents frowned upon.

The group headed back to their rooms, eating their snacks along the way. They said goodnight to each other and went into their rooms.

CHAPTER 6

Once Riley walked into the room she shared with her mom, she overheard her mom on the phone talking quietly.

"Riley has no idea," she heard her mom whisper.

Riley quietly closed the door to their room and tiptoed toward the bathroom, where she figured she could hide out and listen to her mom's conversation. She wanted to know what her mom was talking about.

As she inched closer to the bathroom, she tripped over a bag on the floor and fell to the ground, knocking over the ice bucket that sat on the edge of the counter.

"Riley?" her mom asked.

"Yes, mom, it's me," said Riley, as she picked herself up off the ground.

"Oh, I didn't hear you come in," she said as she put down her cell phone.

Riley was bummed she missed the opportunity to hear what her mom was talking about, but she was also super tired and just wanted to get to bed.

Next door in Nico's room, his parents were sitting out on the balcony when he walked inside.

"Come outside, Nico," his mom yelled to him through the open door. "We are looking at the stars."

Nico ventured outside to sit with his parents, wondering why the door to the balcony was open.

"Should I leave the door open?" he asked.

"We just had it open so we could listen for you," his mom explained. "Plus, it is a beautiful night in the Tennessee mountains. The fresh air flowing into the room will be great for sleeping tonight."

"Look, there's the Big Dipper," Nico's dad pointed out.

The family continued to look at the stars for a bit, then went back inside to get ready for bed.

After about an hour of sleeping, Nico's mom heard a noise coming from the half-open closet. She got out of bed, looking over at Nico who was sound asleep on his bed. She opened the closet door all the way and screamed.

Something flew out of the closet and right into her hair. It then freed itself and flew toward the window, hitting the glass with a thud and then continued to fly around the room.

Nico and his dad quickly woke up and jumped into action. Nico turned on the lights and they discovered it was a bat flying around their room.

"Turn the lights off," said his dad. "Bats don't like the light."

"Yes, but if we keep the lights on, maybe the bat will fly back outside where it is dark," Nico said. "Open the door to the balcony!"

Nico's mom quickly opened the door as Nico and his dad used pillows to lightly shoe the bat toward the open door.

"Nico, grab my phone and look up bats," said his dad. "See if you can determine what kind this is, just so we know if it is dangerous or not."

"Oh, great!" yelled his mom. "Now we potentially have a vampire bat circling us?"

"There's no such thing as vampire bats," said Nico. "But let me finish looking this up and I will let you know."

In the meantime, there was a knock at the door.

"Is everything OK in there?" asked Coach Jake.

Nico's mom opened the door and let him in, filling him in on their situation. He had heard Nico's mom scream, as he was in the room next door.

Coach Jake attempted to catch the bat with his baseball hat, but his attempt failed. A few minutes later, after a lamp was knocked over, Riley and her mom were at the door wondering what was going on. They heard the lamp-crash noise from their room.

Riley's mom called down to the front desk to see if maintenance had a net or something with which they could catch the bat.

"Nico, what have you learned about bats so far?" his dad asked.

"Well, they are intelligent mammals, according to the Internet," Nico said. "They mostly eat insects, so unless you are a bug, you should be safe from the bat."

"Oh, that is a relief," sighed Nico's mom.

"Unless the bat has rabies and bites you," Nico laughed, as his mom screamed again.

"What kind of bat is it?" asked Riley.

"It is hard to tell because it won't sit still," Nico said. "I can't get a good look at it."

"Well, you don't need to," said Nico's dad. "It just flew back outside."

"Thank goodness," sighed Nico's mom. "I was beginning to think we were going to be up all night."

As Coach Jake, Riley, and her mom went back to their

rooms, Nico's parents cleaned up the mess in their room. Nico kept scrolling through his dad's phone, learning more about bats. He loved learning new things, especially anything related to science.

"I guess we'll need to start checking out books about bats from the library, Nico," laughed his mom. "You've already read and re-read all of the weather books. Bats can be your new passion."

"Ha, ha," Nico laughed sarcastically. "I actually would like to learn more about vampires."

Nico's mom threw a pillow at him and told him to go to sleep.

A few minutes later, Nico's parents turned off the lights and went to bed. Everyone was exhausted from the long day of driving and then the bat fiasco. Just as they were all about to fall asleep, there was a pounding at the door.

"This is the hotel manager," a voice yelled. "I have maintenance here with me. We received a call about a bat."

"What were you saying about being up all night?" Nico's dad teased his mom as he turned on the lights and went to the door.

The next day, everyone met up in the lobby for the hotel's free breakfast.

Nico looked outside and discovered that it had rained overnight, as everything was wet and the leaves on the trees were glistening. He looked up the weather on his phone to see what they could expect while driving today. It looked like clear skies ahead.

Coach Jake was telling Dylan's family about the bat, while Dylan and Jordan teased Nico by waving their hands up and down like the flying mammal.

Once everyone was checked out of the hotel, Coach Jake went back to grab more free food.

"What? We have a long car ride ahead of us," Coach Jake explained as all of the other grownups stared at him. The kids all looked at each other, and then decided to follow Coach Jake.

After about an hour on the road, Nico told his mom that he was hungry again.

"You just ate," she said. "Don't you have any of your free muffins left?"

"Coach Jake ate them all," Nico said, giving Coach Jake a dirty look.

"Sorry, you weren't fast enough," laughed Coach Jake.

Nico's mom just laughed and told Nico, "You've always wanted a brother. Now you know what it feels like to have a sibling."

Riley was busy looking out the window and taking pictures of all the rock formations along the road. She had never driven through the mountains before and was in awe of the natural beauty.

"This view is incredible," she said out loud. "And look at all of these signs about falling rocks. You don't see those in Michigan."

"We're definitely not in Michigan anymore," joked Riley's mom.

CHAPTER 7

Driving through the mountains meant there was beautiful scenery out every window.

The kids had stopped playing on their electronics and just kept turning their heads in every direction, pointing out lime formations and different colors in the rock walls that bordered the freeway.

Nico's dad decided to take a much-needed break from driving and get off at a rest area. Dylan's family was driving right behind them, and Nico's mom texted Dylan's mom about taking a break soon. Almost everyone needed to use the restroom.

As they got out of the two vehicles, everyone stretched their arms and legs. The kids met up with each other to talk about the awesome views along the freeway.

After the boys were done using the restroom, they ran over to look at signs and maps showing pictures of the Smoky

Mountains and listing facts. Nico was especially thrilled to learn more about the natural scenery they were passing through.

Nico's mom tried to line everyone up for a group photo while they were stopped at the rest area. Riley obliged with a smile on her face, while the boys pouted and complained.

"I will take a picture of all of you pouting and post it on social media," warned Nico's mom.

The boys all flashed a quick smile for Nico's mom, who was trained to quickly snap pictures of her son and capture a great photo. The boys even cooperated for a group selfie with all of the grownups as well.

Nico's mom told the kids to then go run around and get out some energy before they got back on the road. They all flocked to a group of trees and instantly started climbing them, trying to see who could get the highest. The leaves were still damp from the overnight rain, so some of their clothing got wet.

Jake led the kids in a session of 'jumping Jakes' again, as well as some walking lunges, arm circles, and burpees.

The grownups went over the navigation apps on their phones and made sure they were on the best route possible. They also talked about when and where they would stop for food and gas next, as well as when they would be able to let their ninja kids have a break from sitting still in the car and getting to move around again.

"Do you think there are families with kids who can actually sit still for more than five minutes at a time?" asked Dylan's mom. "You'd think that letting them play on their electronics in the car would satisfy them for a while."

"I wouldn't know," laughed Nico's mom. "I've heard rumors that not all kids have the need to climb on every tree, or every wall for that matter, that they come across. Unless of course it is in a video game."

"I'm glad my kids aren't obsessed with video games, but I don't mind them playing video games on their electronics while we are in the car for hours at a time," laughed Dylan's mom.

The kids then slowly piled back into their vehicles, bummed that they were going to be forced to sit still again for a few hours on the road.

"Good luck," Nico's mom whispered to Dylan's mom.

"Same to you," whispered Dylan's mom. "We'll see who can go the longest without complaining."

The ninja moms laughed as they closed their car doors and ventured back on the road.

The twists and turns and ups and downs through the mountain roads were not only new to the kids, but to the grownups driving as well.

"These roads are crazy," Nico's mom said to his dad. "I don't know how you can navigate them so smoothly."

"I know," agreed Riley's mom. "I was going to offer to take a shift driving, but I think I'll wait until we get to Florida. I'm not used to these mountain roads."

"At least there isn't any snow on them," said Nico's dad. "That would make things interesting."

"Did someone say snow?" Coach Jake asked.

"Relax, Jake," laughed Nico's dad. "There is no snow. Nico told me you'd be looking for it, though."

"You're a poet and you don't know it," Nico joked.

"That was really cheesy, Nico," Riley said.

"Why did you have to say cheese?" Coach Jake asked. "Now I'm hungry again. There is no cheese and no snow. How much longer until we stop again?"

Nico's mom threw a bag of pretzels onto Coach Jake's lap.

"This ought to hold you for a little while," she laughed.

All of a sudden, there was a loud banging noise behind them. Everyone turned around to look and see what made that awful noise. Nico's dad, who was still driving, looked in his rearview mirror in time to see what everyone else had just discovered. Rocks were falling onto the road behind them.

"Rock slide!" shouted Nico.

"Drive faster!" shouted Riley.

"Keep calm, everyone," said Nico's mom. "Don't startle the driver. He will navigate us out of here safely."

She looked over at Nico's dad, who suddenly had sweat on his forehead and worry in his eyes. She knew he was just as nervous as her about the situation they were in, but neither wanted to scare the kids.

Riley's mom called 911 on her cell phone to report the rock slide and ask for help on getting through safely.

Coach Jon, who was driving his family's car next to them, glanced over at Nico's dad and they both exchanged worried glances. Nico's mom quickly called Dylan's mom, who was sitting in the front seat next to Coach Jon. She informed them of the call to 911 and relayed all information she gathered from Riley's mom, who remained on the call with a 911 dispatcher. They were sending emergency vehicles to the area.

Another loud crash occurred behind them. The kids were frozen with fear. They had never experienced something like this. Coach Jake tried to comfort them, as best he could.

"It'll be OK," he told Riley and Nico. "Your parents are all handling this situation like pros."

"What if a rock hits our car?" Riley asked.

"Even worse, what if a boulder hits our car?" Nico asked.

"A boulder could be big enough to take out the entire car," said Riley.

Coach Jake tried not to laugh at Nico and Riley, who kept increasing their list of potential dangers during the emergency situation. It actually helped keep him calm.

"Just think of this as an obstacle course that your dad has to drive through," said Coach Jake. "And think how cool it would be to rock climb around here, you know, without the falling rocks and stuff."

Emergency vehicles were quickly on the scene to block the road for other cars to avoid the area. Nico's dad and Coach Jon, with the guidance of the 911 dispatcher, were both able to pull safely off the road at the next exit.

A police vehicle arrived moments later and an officer approached their cars. They wanted to ensure everyone was OK, and informed them that the rock slide was minor. No cars were hit by the falling rocks, thanks to their quick 911 call.

CHAPTER 8

The families decided after their big scare that it would be a great time to take a driving break and get lunch.

They decided on a fast-food restaurant since it was in the next parking lot.

"Not really a fan of fast food, but I suppose I can get a salad," complained Dylan's mom.

"Well, we aren't going to make everyone happy at every stop," laughed Coach Jon. "You are just as bad as the kids."

Jordan was super excited to go to a fast-food place because he wanted the toy with the kids' meal. He looked at the menu and discovered that the current toy was actually a book.

"A book? Bummer," whined Jordan. "I wanted a toy."

"Jordan, a book is a great prize. And it would be perfect for the car ride," laughed his mom. "You already finished the books we brought with us."

"What kind of books do they have?" Riley asked curiously. She scanned over the menu to look for a photo.

"It looks like a book about soccer," said Nico. "Why can't anyone write a book about ninja warriors and obstacle courses?"

"I agree," sighed Riley. "But this book looks decent. I think I'll get a kids' meal so I have more reading material for the car."

Once they sat to eat, Nico looked up rock slides on his phone. He informed everyone that the recent rain may have contributed to the problem. He explained how rock slides occur and how often.

Coach Jon, who had a list of ninja warrior gyms along their route to Florida, whispered to all of the parents that they were close to Ninja Mountain. Ninja Mountain was well-known in the ninja warrior world for their difficult obstacle courses and gigantic rock wall.

"This would be a good opportunity to get in some training for the kids and take their mind off the rock slide," said Coach Jon.

All of the parents and Coach Jake agreed that Ninja Mountain was a great idea. They told the kids they had a surprise for them, which caught Riley's attention.

"Nico, maybe this is the surprise my mom was talking about," she whispered to her friend.

When Coach Jon announced their plans to spend a couple of hours at Ninja Mountain, the kids were thrilled. Dylan did a flip in the restaurant, which was not well received by his parents.

"Please save the flips for the ninja gym," Coach Jon scolded.

The gym was located about 15 minutes off their route, but the parents knew it would be worth making the detour. The kids would get to let out some bottled-up energy in their favorite environment while training for the TV competition that was just days away.

When they pulled up to Ninja Mountain, the kids shrieked with excitement in the back seat. The thought of going to a new ninja warrior gym was like Christmas for ninja kids. They had no idea what awaited them inside the building.

Their hopes and dreams were met when they saw the set up inside the gym. There were obstacles hanging everywhere, including wing nuts and trapeze-style bars. Along the entire back half of the building was the infamous, gigantic rock wall designed for rock climbing and bouldering.

"That looks much safer than the boulders along the road," laughed Coach Jake.

"Look, there is the Big Dipper," Dylan said excitedly,

pointing to a huge obstacle. "That took out some of the ninja pros on *The Ultimate Ninja Competition* last year."

"That is way cooler than the Big Dipper we saw in the sky last night," laughed Nico.

The Big Dipper is an obstacle that has ninjas grasping a metal bar and sliding down a track, then releasing the bar in time to grab a rope at the end of the track.

The kids and grownups were all in awe of Ninja Mountain.

Riley thanked her mom for surprising her with the trip to the gym.

"What do you mean?" asked her mom.

"I knew you were hiding a surprise," Riley confessed. "I overheard you talking on the phone, but didn't hear the part about the ninja gym. This place is amazing!"

"Oh, that. Wait, you were spying on me?" her mom asked accusingly.

"Sorry mom, it was sort of accidental," she admitted. "But this was the surprise you were referring to, right?"

"Yep, that was it," her mom laughed.

She couldn't reveal what the real surprise was to Riley and realized that she needed to be more cautious of phone calls regarding the secret. She was glad her daughter had no idea that something much bigger was coming.

Riley joined the boys on the obstacle course. She ran right to the trapeze bars, anxious to hang and stretch out her body.

Coach Jake joined the kids on the course, making sure everyone did warmups and stretches before they continued onto the obstacles. Then they all anxiously ventured on to every ninja obstacle they possibly could.

The parents met with the owner of the gym, Coach Charlotte, whom they have met at competitions in the past. She was happy to show them around and offered coffee to the grownups, who looked really worn out.

"You wouldn't believe the trip we've had so far," Nico's mom explained to Coach Charlotte. She told her all about the bat in the hotel room and the rock-slide scare.

Nico and Riley met a girl named Allie who was working on laches on the trapeze bars. They told her they were in town for the afternoon but then would be continuing on their road trip to Orlando for *The Ultimate Kid Ninja Competition*. Allie told the kids that she was headed to Orlando tomorrow for the same competition. Her twin brother, Luke, was also competing in the event.

Allie pointed to the kid who was running up a warped wall and said, "That's Luke."

Nico noticed that Dylan was running up the warped wall next to Luke and it looked like they were racing. He headed over to check out the action.

"I won!" Dylan shouted from the top of the wall. Luke reached the top of his wall just seconds later.

"Hey Dylan," Nico yelled, pointing over to Luke. "He's going to the TV competition, too."

Allie and Riley joined the boys and introduced them to each other once everyone was back on the ground. Luke was taller than Dylan, but Dylan knew his height wouldn't be much of an issue. He just beat him on the warped wall, after all.

"I see you've all met each other," said Coach Charlotte, who was followed by Nico's parents, Riley's mom, Dylan's parents, and Coach Jake.

"So, you are the kids who are headed to Orlando, too?" asked Coach Jon, speaking to Allie and Luke. "Coach Charlotte said you are both great competitors."

"It looks like you've got some great athletes as well," said Coach Charlotte. "Good luck to all of you."

Nico, Riley, Dylan, and Jordan managed to try out every obstacle at Ninja Mountain before they left. Coach Jake managed to do every obstacle, plus climb the entire rock wall. Coach Jon joined his kids on the obstacle course for a bit and then climbed the rock wall with Coach Jake.

"Hope you are all worn out and will sleep for your long car ride," Coach Charlotte teased as they headed out the door.

"No chance of that happening," laughed Nico's dad. "We

can't wear these ninja kids out no matter what."

"I know the type," laughed Coach Charlotte. "See y'all in Orlando!"

"Welcome to Florida!" Nico and Riley shouted from the back seat as they read the sign at the border.

After a couple of long days of driving, they were finally in the Sunshine State, which is the nickname for Florida. The kids' excitement faded, though, once their parents told them they still had a couple of hours to drive to Orlando.

"Well, at least now we can look at palm trees along our route," said Nico's mom, as she cracked open her window to let in the warm, fresh air. "I could get used to this every day."

CHAPTER 9

The archway in front of the hotel complex where all of the competitors for *The Ultimate Kid Ninja Competition* were staying had a huge banner reading, "Welcome, ninjas!"

"We made it!" Nico yelled.

"Finally!" added Riley.

"I don't think I could stand sitting next to you for one more minute," joked Coach Jake.

"You aren't exactly the best person to sit by in a car, you know," said Nico.

While the adults checked in to the hotel, the kids promised to stick together to explore the complex. There was a huge, rectangular pool and a splash pad, both perfect for cooling off in the hot, Florida sun. There was an arcade, a gift shop, and a restaurant. The hotel area was neat and all, but the kids were even more excited to see the obstacle course for *The Ultimate Kid Ninja Competition.*

"When do we go to the ninja course?" Nico asked his dad as they met back up in the lobby.

"Not until tomorrow," explained his dad. "Nobody gets an early peek at the course. You will see it tomorrow for the competition just like everyone else."

"I can't wait one more day!" Nico whined.

"Well, you don't have a choice," said his mom. "We will have a fun afternoon, though, of meeting up with the other kids in the competition for pizza by the pool."

"I guess that would be fine," said Nico, smirking.

When it was time to meet up for the pool party, Nico and Riley ran out of their hotel rooms and down the long hallway.

"Don't run, especially in flip flops," yelled Nico's mom. "I don't want you to twist your ankles before the competition tomorrow."

Nico and Riley had spotted their friends Joey and Megan from Great Obstacles. They flew down to Orlando with their families, along with a few other families from the Midwest region.

"Can you believe this place?" Joey asked. "I want to climb a palm tree!"

"I want to jump in the pool," laughed Nico, as he pushed past his friend toward the pool, where he made a huge splash. "Cannonball!"

Inside the pool area, there were tables and chairs set up for the party, along with a long table of pizzas, salads, and fresh Florida oranges. The staff made sure there was enough food for everyone and that the lifeguards remained on duty until the party was over.

Coach Daniel surprised the kids by showing up at the pool party. He was able to get away last minute, so he took a flight and arrived in time to help prepare the kids for the competition.

As much fun as everyone had at the pool, the coaches and parents told the kids they had to head back to their rooms early. All of the ninjas competing tomorrow would need a good night's sleep. The kids didn't complain too much because they were excited for the next day's competition.

Shuttle buses lined up along the curb of the hotel in the morning, waiting to take the ninja kids, their families, and their coaches to the set of *The Ultimate Kid Ninja Competition*.

Nico and his family wore the Ninja Nico shirts that his mom had made. Coach Daniel and Coach Jake had several shirts in their hands, as they had one to represent and cheer on each of the kids from their gym.

One of those kids was Riley, who finally had a ninja shirt of her own. Riley's mom made purple shirts with a smiley face and the nickname the "Smiley Ninja" labeled in bright pink. She knew the colors on her shirt were considered girly, but she was proud to be a girl ninja.

Riley has had the nickname from her dad of "Smiley Riley" from the time she was a baby. Since her dad was away this past year while Riley started ninja training, she and her mom thought it would be a thoughtful way to include her dad on her ninja quest.

Nico and Riley, both proudly wearing their own ninja shirts, looked around at the other competitors. They recognized a few faces from past competitions and some shirts bearing ninja nicknames that they knew from social media. They even spotted Allie and Luke from Ninja Mountain.

"Good luck today," the kids yelled to each other.

Another face caught Riley's eye as she scanned the crowd. She thought her mind was playing tricks on her, until she heard a very familiar voice.

"There's my Smiley Riley!" shouted a man wearing a Smiley Ninja shirt.

"Daddy!?" yelled Riley, who was in complete shock. "What are you doing here?"

"Surprise!" shouted her mom. "Now this was my secret."

Riley hugged her dad tightly. She hadn't seen him in a year and missed him terribly.

"I missed you so much," Riley cried to her dad.

As tears filled her eyes, warmth filled her heart. She had waited so long for this moment.

"I missed you, baby girl," he said back to Riley, wiping the tears in both of their eyes.

"I can't believe you are here! You are here for my competition!" Riley yelled excitedly.

"I wasn't sure if I'd make it in time, so I told your mom not to say anything," he explained. "And the look on your face right now is priceless, especially that smile. My Smiley Riley."

Riley hugged her dad again and felt as if now her world was complete. She had her whole family together for one of the biggest moments of her life. The smile on her face reflected the smile on her shirt and she was ready to conquer the world, or at least the TV ninja course.

Nico anxiously entered the gated entrance to the outdoor complex where *The Ultimate Kid Ninja Competition* would be held.

The giant obstacle course that stood in front of Nico was bigger and better than he had even dreamed. The structure glimmered in the Florida sunshine.

"I can't believe we are here!" yelled Nico.

"It's been a long road," said his dad. "And I'm not just talking about the car ride. You have been working hard for this moment and I'm proud of you. Now, let's go show off your skills!"

The obstacle course was set up in one long row, just like on *The Ultimate Ninja Competition* show. Nico couldn't wait to fly through the course, which consisted of lache bars, swinging ropes, the Flying Squirrel (two swingable handles that the contestant laches from and grasps another set of handles), several wing nuts, and of course a warped wall. The wall for the kids in his age group was at 14 feet, which luckily Nico had mastered this past year.

Nico saw some of his friends from his home gym, along with new friends he met at the gym in Tennessee. There were also lots of new faces of kids who lived all over the country. The butterflies in Nico's stomach seemed to triple in size and he wondered if everyone was as nervous as him.

The best way to work out his nerves was to do what he did best, and that was being a ninja warrior. The TV show had a workout area set up for contestants with some slack lines and teeter-totter-like balance boards. There were bars overhead for the kids to practice their laches and work on their grips. A giant rock wall bordered the edge of the workout area, and Nico thought about the rock slide they experienced on their road trip. He was glad these rocks were bolted on the wall.

As Nico's eyes wandered the workout area, he spotted Riley and Dylan working on their laches. He watched as his ninja friends flew through the air from bar to bar and saw how much fun they were having.

"I have nothing to be nervous about," Nico thought to himself. "The ninja course is my favorite place to be."

He felt a surge of confidence and happiness run through his body as he lached from bar to bar. The Florida sunshine also helped uncloud any negative thoughts in his head and helped his nerves relax.

After a nice warm-up session on the ninja course, Nico and his ninja friends and family sat in the spectator seats to listen to the producers talk about the plan for the competition. Nico and Riley recognized a familiar face, producer Jessie Knight, who was present at Great Obstacles on the day they competed for their spot on the TV show. She seemed to be in charge of everything as she went over an agenda.

Joining her on stage were a few stars from the grownup show – Maggie "The Meteor" Drew and Ryan "Lache" Scott – who were a couple of the best ninja warrior competitors of all time. They have won *The Ultimate Ninja Competition* three times each and were both well-known for conquering ninja courses at gyms across the country. They love to interact with fans on social media and were really active in the ninja warrior community.

"No way!" shrieked Riley. "That's Ryan Scott! He is going to be hosting?"

"It looks that way," laughed Nico, who knew Riley was a huge fan of the ninja warrior star.

Maggie and Ryan spoke to the crowd of competitors, their families, and their coaches about the course and how it would be slightly altered for each age group. They explained the obstacles in a walk-through of the course. Maggie and Ryan even demonstrated a few obstacles, which the crowd loved.

"They are even cooler in person," gushed Riley about the ninja stars.

"They are people, just like you and me," said Riley's mom.

"No, they are *ninjas*, just like you and *me*," chimed in Nico.

There were three age groups for the competitors: Level 1, Level 2, and Level 3. Jordan was in Level 1 with the younger kids, while Nico, Riley, Dylan, and their ninja friends were in Level 2. Level 3 mostly consisted of teenagers.

When Jessie announced that Level 1 was the first group to compete, Jordan instantly became nervous.

"We have to go first?" he cried.

"Going in the first group means you get to go on the

obstacle course sooner than Dylan, and then you'll be done and can relax the rest of the day," said his mom, comforting him.

"You got this, bro," said Dylan, giving his little brother a fist bump.

Nico, Riley, and everyone from their road trip gathered to cheer on Jordan and the other contestants. They were surrounded by other ninja families and coaches, who also cheered on all of the competitors.

The sport of ninja warrior has a very positive environment, where everyone cheers each other on, even those who they are competing against. It was great to watch competitors reach their personal best and overcome obstacles that have challenged them in the past.

Jordan had a great run for his age group, but only completed five of the eight obstacles on the course. There were several kids who completed all eight obstacles, so he knew he wouldn't place in the top three. He was disappointed at first, but saw his fans cheering for him in the crowd and instantly felt better. And now he could enjoy the rest of the day cheering on Dylan and his friends.

When it was time for the Level 2 kids to compete, Nico looked at Riley and they both smiled at each other. Who would have thought two kids who played on a backyard obstacle course would now be competing on a course that would be on national TV?

"We got this," Riley said to Nico, as she ran over to her parents for one more hug.

"We are so proud of you, Ninja Nico," said his parents, as they met up for a hug also.

"Have fun and do your best," said his mom and dad in sync.

Nico looked at the course, which had been slightly modified to be more challenging for the Level 2 kids, and took in a deep breath. This was the moment he had been waiting for since he was a little kid watching *The Ultimate Ninja Competition* on TV.

CHAPTER 10

Back to present day ...

"So, did you win?" blurted out Nico's grandma as she stared at the TV screen.

"You'll just have to keep watching," Nico laughed. "Level 2 is up next."

Nico, Riley, and their family, friends, and coaches were gathered around the TV in the family room at Nico's house, watching the two-hour special of *The Ultimate Kid Ninja Competition* together.

Nico and Riley made obstacles out of pillows and the kitchen chairs that Nico's dad brought in for extra seating. Coach Jake joined in on the fun by doing a headstand.

"Some things never change," Nico's dad laughed.

"Who would have thought that my little guy who used to climb on all of the furniture while we watched *The Ultimate*

Ninja Competition on TV, would now be a 10-year-old climbing on the furniture watching himself on the TV!" laughed Nico's mom.

"Quiet!" yelled Nico's grandma. "The show is back from commercial."

"There's me and Nico!" Riley yelled, pointing to the TV. "We were in that group of kids who were warming up on the lache bars."

"Wow, to think that I knew you both before you were TV stars," joked Jacob.

Nico threw a pillow at him as everyone's attention went back to the TV.

There were lots of familiar faces on the screen for the Level 2 group, especially every time they showed the cheering crowd. Nico's mom pointed out who everyone was to Nico's grandparents and family, since they weren't as familiar with the ninja warrior family.

"Those bright purple and pink Smiley Ninja shirts really stand out, and so do the orange Ninja Nico shirts," Riley's mom said proudly. "We did a good job on them."

Nico's mom gave her a fist bump and the kids started cracking up.

When it was time for Riley's run on the course, everyone went quiet again.

Smiley Riley, the Smiley Ninja, started off strong on the Level 2 course, which consisted of:

- Slanted quintuple steps
- Pegboard
- Cargo net
- Swinging ropes
- Flying Squirrel
- Balance log over a pool of water
- Wing nuts
- 14-foot warped wall

Riley was an expert at the pegboard because there was one on Nico's backyard ninja course. Everyone watching the TV cringed, though, when her foot got caught in the cargo net. Riley had remained calm, recovered, and continued on the course.

"This is a nail biter," Riley's mom said.

"Mom, you were there and know what happens," laughed Riley.

"I know I was there, and it was a nail biter then and a nail biter now," added Riley's mom.

"And I am so glad I was able to witness the competition and be here for the TV viewing," said Riley's dad, tearing up. "I'm so proud of you, Smiley Riley."

Riley hugged her dad as they finished watching her run on TV. Her mom joined in for a group hug.

Riley was able to make it through all of the obstacles, until she met the 14-foot warped wall, which she had not been able to reach at Great Obstacles and the local ninja gyms. She looked intently at the structure like she was staring up at a mountain. She remembered the beautiful mountains she had seen on the road trip and thought she could handle this wall. Then she thought about the falling rocks they witnessed and she started having her doubts.

"What was going through your mind, Riley?" asked Nico's grandma as she watched the TV closely.

"Oh, just how I was gonna 'rock' on that wall," laughed Riley.

As Riley attempted to run up the wall, Coach Daniel and Coach Jake could be seen giving support along the sidelines. They were shouting so loud that their voices could actually be heard on the TV.

After the allotted three attempts on the wall, Riley was unable to reach the top.

There was a collective sigh in Nico's family room as everyone watched Riley walk off the course.

"Good job, Riley," everyone said encouragingly.

"Thank you," Riley answered back. "I was bummed, but I had a lot of fun being on a TV show. I just couldn't conquer that mountain. And I will continue to work on the 14-foot wall at Great Obstacles."

A few other ninja kids that Nico's family knew took their turns flying across the obstacle course on the TV screen. Joey and Megan from Great Obstacles each made it more than halfway across the course. As did two other kids from the Midwest region, Hunter and Olivia, who had earned spots on the show at the Great Obstacles competition.

Allie and Luke from Ninja Mountain in Tennessee each finished the course in just over three minutes. Luke had a little trouble on the wing nuts, which used up a lot of his time. Allie took several tries on the warped wall, with finally reaching the top on her third and final attempt.

"Now that girl can conquer a mountain!" Riley yelled, proud of her new ninja friend.

One of the shining stars of the TV competition was Dylan. He tackled the course faster than most of the other kids. He was able to complete the whole thing in just under three minutes.

A ninja kid named Donnie, who was from Boston, Massachusetts, nearly tied Dylan. He was just a little bit faster and finished in 2 minutes and 55 seconds. That knocked Dylan out of first place.

Another star of the obstacle course was a kid named Jack, who was from Windsor, Connecticut. He also finished the course and did it faster than Donnie at 2 minutes and 46 seconds.

Nico was the last competitor of the Level 2 age group. He

was glad he was able to watch everyone's runs and cheer them on. Now it was his turn to shine.

Butterflies rapidly flew in his stomach and sweat dripped from his body in the hot Florida sun. He wiped his face and hands with a towel. Then he wiped off the bottom of his shoes one more time before he hit the course, making sure he had as much traction as possible.

While watching him prepare on the TV screen, Nico's grandma told him she was proud of him win or lose.

"Hopefully it is a win," joked his grandpa.

Nico's parents stared at the TV screen with pride. They knew the outcome and did their best to conceal their feelings so they didn't ruin it for Nico's grandparents, aunt, uncle, cousins, and friends who were not at the TV show taping.

Everyone cheered as they watched Nico run through the course on the TV screen. He flew past the first couple of obstacles, as he was familiar with each of them. When it came to the Flying Squirrel, he was a little nervous, as he wasn't as familiar with this obstacle. He pushed through his nerves, though, and completed the obstacle quickly and successfully. He ran across the balance log with ease and flew through the air on the wing nuts. He knew he needed to not only complete the course, but do it faster than Jack if he wanted to win.

Without hesitation, Nico ran as fast as he could up the 14-

foot warped wall. He used every muscle in his legs to push himself further and further up the wall. His ninja shoes had perfect traction, and he stretched up his arms as high as he could to grab the top of the wall. Once he had a grip on the wall, he pulled up the rest of his body, swinging his legs to propel them higher and faster. He slammed his hand down on the red buzzer and looked for his time on the clock. He had finished in 2 minutes and 46 seconds. He had tied with Jack.

"What? A tie?" Nico's grandma yelled at the TV screen.

"Don't worry, Grandma, there is more to come," Nico laughed.

His cousins Anna and Sydney were screaming at the TV when it went to commercial break. They were dying to know if Nico won or not.

When the show resumed, there was a tiebreaker set up for Nico and Jack. They each had a rope hanging from a beam with a buzzer attached to the top. They needed to race each other and whoever reached the buzzer first was the winner.

Nico and Jack fist bumped each other before they got started. Coach Daniel and Coach Jake both gave Nico a quick consult on how to handle the rope. Everyone in the crowd cheered on both kids as the countdown started.

When they heard the horn sound, Nico and Jack climbed as fast as they could up the rope. Nico swiftly pulled himself toward the top, using all of his strength and a leg technique that his coaches had taught him at Great Obstacles.

Nico knew Jack was a little bit longer than him, so he would have to work just a little harder to reach the top of the rope. As soon as he felt he was close enough, he stretched up his arm and hit the buzzer. He beat Jack. He was *The Ultimate Kid Ninja Competition* winner!

"Nico won!" shouted his grandma and cousins as they watched his big win on TV.

"Awesome!" yelled Jacob and Ryder.

As everyone celebrated his big finish, Nico felt the love from his family. He also felt a little pain when he was tackled by his friends. Coach Jake joined in because he couldn't miss an opportunity to tackle someone.

Coach Mia was the only coach at Great Obstacles who didn't know the outcome of the show.

"Great job, Ninja Nico!" she said proudly. "You really put Great Obstacles on the ninja map."

"We are hanging up your Ninja Nico shirt at the gym," said Coach Daniel. "And we'll put the Smiley Ninja's shirt up next to it."

Riley's coaches were so proud of her for all she had accomplished. She went from a beginner to *The Ultimate Kid Ninja Competition* in a short amount of time.

Nobody was prouder than her dad, though. He swung her

up in his arms and squeezed her tight.

Nico's family surrounded him with hugs and high fives. He suddenly flew into the air, though, and landed on the shoulders of Coach Jake.

"Ninja Nico, you are the ultimate kid ninja warrior!" he shouted.

Nico felt like he was on top of the ninja warrior world.

ABOUT THE AUTHOR

From creative writing awards as a child to a career as an online news writer and editor, writing has always been a part of Marcy's life.

She loves to blog about pop culture and parenting, as well as write children's books. Her two kids, Nico and Mia, are both ninja warriors and have inspired Marcy's stories with their strengths, abilities, and dreams.

Marcy lives in suburbia with her husband, kids, and dogs.

The entire Ninja Nico book series is available on Amazon and Kindle. You can find more information on this series and other works by the author at MarcyNicole.com.

1. *Ninja Nico and the Secret Ninja*
2. *Ninja Nico and the Zombie Fest*
3. *Ninja Nico and the Storm*
4. *Ninja Nico: Ultimate Ninja Warrior Road Trip*

Made in the USA
Monee, IL
29 April 2021